School Is A Nightmare #2
The Field Trip

RAYMOND BEAN

ISBN: 1469949776
ISBN 13: 9781469949772

www.raymondbean.com

Raymond Bean books

<u>Sweet Farts Series</u>
Sweet Farts #1
Sweet Farts #2 Rippin' It Old School
Sweet Farts #3 Blown Away
(Coming April 3, 2012)

<u>School Is A Nightmare Series</u>
School Is A Nightmare #1
First Week, Worst Week
School Is A Nightmare #2 The Field Trip
School Is A Nightmare #3
(Coming Summer 2012)

For Stacy, Ethan, and Chloe.

Interested in scheduling an
author visit or web based author talk?
Email us at raymondbeanbooks@gmail.com

Contents

1
Snake Bite

The morning of the field trip, I woke up early. Mom and Dad had given my pet snake away a week earlier, and I couldn't get him out of my head. They gave him away because he got out of his cage and scared my sister Becky half to death on the first day of school. Somehow he managed to get into the bathroom cabinet. She got so freaked out when she found him that she sprayed him with hair spray. When I rushed in to save him, I accidentally knocked her, hands first, into the toilet.

His name is Mr. Squeeze, and he is by far the coolest snake in the whole world! My parents didn't care, though. To them he was just a pain-in-the-neck pet that was causing trouble in their lives. If it were up to me, we would have given Becky away instead.

As bad as it was that Becky fell in the toilet, it was only part of the reason they sent Mr. Squeeze packing. It was when I threw a packet of powdered soup mix on my sister Mindy while she was in the shower that really sealed Mr. Squeeze's fate.

Poor Mr. Squeeze has spent every day since at Dad's friend Paul's house. Unfortunately for me and Mr. Squeeze, Paul hasn't been enjoying taking care of a boa constrictor as much as he'd hoped. He told Dad he'd only keep the snake for a few weeks. After that, he'd have to give it back to us, or we'd have to give it to a pet shop. My parents told me that we were not bringing him back home. The thought of someone else getting to keep my snake was driving me bananas.

It was five in the morning. We weren't leaving for the field trip until about six forty-five, and I was wide awake.

It was a perfect morning for finding snakes. The sun would be up soon, and it was really warm out. Mom said I couldn't keep Mr. Squeeze. She also said I couldn't buy a new snake. But, she never said anything about *finding* a new snake.

The trail behind our house leads right into the woods. If you know where to look, there are always some snakes hiding. I'm not sure why I love snakes so much, but I always have. I don't understand why people like my sisters are so afraid of them. Unless they have venom, they're completely harmless.

I checked all the places I've found snakes. Usually I find Garter snakes. They like to hide in piles of rocks or wood. It didn't take long before I found a pretty big one hiding behind a tree stump. I saw the tail first. It was next to a root and blending perfectly. To an inexperienced snake hunter, it would have looked like just a root, but I'm not inexperienced. I pounced on it, grabbing the tail. It immediately twisted to get away. Then it turned back faster than I expected and bit me on the right hand.

The bite was on that meaty part of my hand between the thumb and pointer finger. Garter snakes are harmless, but their bite stings like crazy. It also itches. I've been bitten a bunch of times, so I wasn't freaked out or anything. I grabbed at him again with my left hand and then slid my right hand up his neck to get hold of his head. He opened his mouth to try to get at me, but the fight was over.

I stuck him in the bag I had brought with me. In all the nature shows I watch, the explorer always sticks the snake in a bag. It works great because they get all calm. It's a pretty awesome feeling catching a snake.

I was about to start looking for another one when I heard my mom's voice echo through the trees. "Justin! Are you back there? We need to leave for your trip! We're late!"

I looked at my watch and realized I'd been out looking for snakes for over an hour. It was already after seven, and the bus was set to leave from school at seven thirty. I'd been looking forward to the field trip all week, and I didn't want to miss the bus.

"Where were you?" Mom asked when I raced into the backyard. "The girls and I have been looking all over the place."

"I was in the woods," I said.

"I can see that. You look filthy. Get inside and clean up, and please tell me you took a shower already?"

"No shower yet," I said, running for the back door. "I'll take one after the trip. We need to go."

"At least wash your face. And get your lunch out of the fridge and put it in your backpack!" she said, running after me.

2
Lunch?

I put the snake in Mr. Squeeze's extra tank, which was in my closet, turned on the heat lamp, and dropped a few crickets in. Then I placed the screen on top, grabbed my backpack, and sprinted for the car. I knew it would be a close call to make the bus. Mrs. Cliff, my teacher, definitely would not wait for us. At seven thirty, that bus was going to leave, with or without me.

We were headed to the Statue of Liberty, the Brooklyn Bridge, and Times Square. We were only two weeks into the new school year, and I was ready for summer vacation. This trip was going to be the perfect break from school.

When I got to the car, Becky and Mindy were already waiting in the backseat. Our car is a really small Honda Civic, and when we all have to get in together, it's way too crowded. I usually end up sitting in the middle because I'm the youngest, and they love getting the window seats. Today I was jammed in the middle, as usual.

Being with my mom in the morning can be pretty stressful. She's always in a huge rush. If you didn't know any better, you might think she was being chased by villains or something.

We were halfway to school. It was ten minutes after seven when Becky grabbed my hand and asked, "What happened to you?"

Mindy took one look at my bite and slapped my hand away. "That's soo gross!"

"What's the matter?" Mom asked, looking back from the front seat.

"It's nothing," I said. "I got bitten in the woods. That's all."

"Ew! It looks like it's a rat bite," Becky said confidently.

"How would you know what a rat bite looks like?"

"What was it then?" Mom asked.

"It was just a small snake. I'm fine."

"You tell me twenty minutes before we're about to get on a bus to New York City that you were bitten by a snake?"

"Oh my God!" Mindy said. "You're going to die. Mom, we have to go to the hospital!"

"I'm not going to die."

"I'm calling the doctor," Mom announced.

She scrolled through her phone to find the doctor's phone number, and it hit me. I had forgotten my lunch. We were going on an all-day trip to the city, and I had nothing to eat.

"Mom," I interrupted.

"I'm on the phone, Justin!" she said.

"I kind of forgot my lunch at home," I whispered.

"Don't kid around. I told you before we left to grab your lunch from the fridge."

"Yeah…like I said, I forgot my lunch at home."

3
Gas Station Sambo

Mom pulled into a gas station parking lot as if we were fueling up for a NASCAR pit stop. She was still on hold with the doctor, so she sent me into the convenience store of the gas station to get a sandwich.

"Really?" I asked. "You want me to get a sandwich from a gas station?"

"Go!" she demanded

The girls stayed with Mom and worried about my bite. I looked at the pathetic sandwich choices in the display case. All of them looked pretty nasty, but I knew I needed to get something. It was going to be a long day, and Mrs. Cliff had been very clear that no one would be buying unnecessary items on the trip. She said that if we wanted to spend our money in New York City, we could go back with our parents one day. When we were with her, we were not to buy anything, and that included food.

I heard a kid bought a hot dog on the trip last year, from one of those guys selling them on the street, and Mrs. Cliff slapped it out of his hands. They say it splattered all over the sidewalk, and she didn't even say sorry. I wasn't sure if I should believe it, but I wasn't about to find out firsthand. Her message was clear: no buying stuff on the trip.

I was already on Mrs. Cliff's bad side ever since I fell into her prize collection of antique glass marbles the first week of school. She'd had them for about a thousand years, and I ended up breaking them. She was definitely holding a grudge, and I didn't need any more problems.

I'm a pretty picky eater. So buying a gas station sandwich was not something I enjoyed. In fact, it completely grossed me out. The thought of where the sandwiches came from was enough to make me gag. I'd seen a reality TV show once that followed food from the warehouse all the way to the store. After seeing that show, I was sure whatever sandwich I picked had been handled by more germ-covered hands and disgusting creepy-crawlies than I could imagine. Mom honked her horn and waved for me to come. I closed my eyes and grabbed the first sandwich I touched. The label read Ham and Mayo Sambo. *What can you do?* I thought. I paid for my gross sandwich and hurried to the car.

"What were you doing in there?" Mom asked.

"They all looked gross. I couldn't decide."

"We're going to miss the bus," Mindy announced.

"What do you mean by 'we'?" I asked. "This is my trip."

The girls both smiled. "It's *our* field trip now! Since you were running so late, Mom doesn't have time to take us to school. We're going to have to go on the trip too," Becky said.

The girls are in fifth and sixth grade, and they go to a different school than me.

"Mom, they're kidding, right?"

"I agreed to chaperone your trip, and the plan was to drop the girls off on the way to your school. I'm sure Mrs. Cliff will understand."

"No, she won't. She specifically said that siblings aren't allowed. She told us that about a trillion times. Please, Mom! There's got to be another way! Mrs. Cliff already doesn't like me very much. This isn't good timing."

4
You're on the Lame Bus

I was still trying to convince Mom that the girls couldn't come as we pulled into the school parking lot. She had stopped listening to me minutes before we arrived.

There were seven classes going on the trip. I was really excited when I saw the coach buses lined up in front of the school. Usually we take the lame old yellow school buses on field trips, but since this was a long trip to New York City, the teachers had booked us the coach buses.

I was psyched because I'd never been on a field trip on a coach bus before. My friend Aaron's older brother told me that coach bus trips are the best. They've got bathrooms and everything. He said kids sneak up into the luggage compartments when the teachers aren't paying attention and hide. On a trip he went on once, a kid climbed up in the luggage compartment and fell asleep. He stayed up there the whole bus ride! I couldn't wait to try it, even though it would be nearly impossible to have any fun with Becky, Mindy, and Mom watching my every move.

As we walked toward the buses, it was very clear that we were late. Mrs. Cliff was the only teacher standing on the sidewalk. She had a clipboard in one hand and a timer in the other. It was exactly seven forty.

I could tell that even Mom was nervous when she said, "Hi, Mrs. Cliff. I'm so sorry we're running late."

"These buses should already be in motion. There's no time for excuses and stories," Mrs.

Cliff said. "Let's get on the bus, and you can tell me *all* about it."

She pointed toward a beat-up old yellow bus parked behind the sparkling coaches. I squinted to get a better look. My class was already on the bus. Mrs. Cliff led us along the sidewalk toward the yellow clunker. Mom explained to her that she was late because I'd been injured, and she had to bring the girls along. Mrs. Cliff didn't seem happy about them coming, but she wanted to get on the buses and get out of there.

I looked up, and my buddy Aaron and a bunch of other guys from my football team were waving out the window of one of the coaches. Aaron mouthed, "What's going on?"

I shrugged my shoulders. It didn't feel real. It wasn't at all how the trip was supposed to be going. I was looking forward to sitting with all my friends, goofing around, waving out the window to weird people in their cars, trying to get truckers to blow their horn. But none of that was going to happen because all my friends were on the awesome bus.

Becky pointed to Mrs. Cliff's bright white sneakers and giggled. I have the exact same pair. The girls had convinced Mom that they were the coolest sneakers when we went school supply shopping. I tried to convince Mom not to buy them, but she bought them anyway. I looked completely ridiculous in them. They were designed for people who want to lose weight and make their butt look good. The heel is larger than any other sneaker I've ever seen before.

"I love that you and Mrs. Cliff have the same taste in sneakers," Becky teased.

"Mrs. Cliff," I interrupted, "how about if my mom and sisters go on the yellow bus and I go on the bus with Mrs. Fiesta's class? I know my friend Aaron was saving me a seat."

She stopped and turned to face me. "I'll have you know that the reason we're all going on the yellow bus, and not a comfortable coach bus with air-conditioning, is because a certain someone couldn't get here on time. Now you want to have all of us ride in the hot, old bus while you ride in comfort?"

They all waited for me to answer. "Well, yeah. That would be awesome."

"Unbelievable," my sisters said at the same time.

"Truly," Mrs. Cliff added.

5
Sit with Your Sisters

The bus was so hot it felt like the air was sweating. "Oh my gosh," my mom said, reaching the top of the steps.

Mrs. Cliff said, "Prepare to sweat."

"Why didn't the teachers order enough coach buses?" Mindy asked in a semi-insulting tone.

"We did order enough coach buses, young lady," Mrs. Cliff said. "However, one of them broke down due to the heat. Since we had one odd class, the teachers agreed that the last class to have all the kids arrive would take the yellow bus. If you'd been on time, we would be on a comfortable bus right now."

The girls and Mom glared at me. I turned and noticed that down the aisle of the bus, all the kids in my class and a bunch of sweaty parents were looking at me too. "Where should I sit, Mrs. Cliff?"

She pointed to the seat right behind hers. "You can sit with your sisters, and I'll sit with your mom."

"Perfect," I said sarcastically. *This is exactly how I imagined*, I thought.

"You better not sweat," Mindy said, sliding into her window seat. "Your armpits already smell, and I have no interest in sniffing that for the next couple of hours."

"You better not die from that cobra bite either," Becky added, making fangs with her teeth.

"It wasn't a cobra bite," I said, sliding into the seat next to Mindy.

The bus driver fired up the old clunker, and we rattled out of the parking lot. I was squished between my sisters and sitting directly behind my mom and my teacher. *This is going to be fun,* I thought. I looked at my watch. It was already 7:50.

6
Ewwwww! A Tick!

We had been driving for about twenty minutes when Mindy screeched like she'd been dropped off a ten-story building. Becky joined right in. I don't know why, but usually when one of my sisters screams or cries, the other one does it too even before knowing why. It's like a reflex they can't control. Their screeches of horror caused Mom and Mrs. Cliff to turn around.

"What's wrong?" Mom shouted.

"Justin!" Mindy stammered.

"What about Justin?" Mom demanded.

All Mindy could manage was another high-pitched screech.

"What is it?" Mrs. Cliff screamed in a voice so loud it thundered through the bus like a sonic boom.

Mindy immediately started to cry, which made Becky cry. The sight and sound of the two of them crying made Mom cry. I realized in all the panic that Mindy kept pointing to my ear, so I put my hand to it and felt a bump.

"I think I have a tick," I said. The thought of some gross insect feeding on my ear blood was pretty gross. I carefully felt where it was attached. It was on pretty good. I tried to pull it off, but it wouldn't budge.

"Leave it alone!" Mom shouted.

Mindy instantly fainted and slumped onto me. I shoved her away and back onto the window. Becky might as well have spontaneously combusted right there on the spot. The sound that came out of her was beyond a shriek, but not quite a scream. It was a sound that I hope to never hear again as long as I live.

"Yeah, I definitely have a tick in my ear," I said. A lot of my friends have had ticks. I've never had one, which is pretty amazing because I spend so much time in the woods.

"Stop the bus!" Mrs. Cliff shouted. "*Stop this bus right now!* Everyone stay completely still! We have a situation!"

7
Don't Get Hit by a Car

I'm not sure if my feet even touched the ground when Mrs. Cliff ripped me from my seat and down the bus stairs. The bus driver stopped on the side of the highway, and the only thing going through my head was that there were cars zooming by at about a hundred miles an hour. The tick behind my ear would be the least of my problems if I was struck by a car.

"Mrs. Cliff?" I asked.

"Yes, Justin?" she asked.

Cars screamed by so fast I could feel their wind. "Do you think this is safe?"

"No, I don't. But I don't think I can possibly get this tick out of your ear with your sisters and mother screaming and crying, so I suggest you stay still before we both get killed."

"All right," I said.

"And for the record, you don't have *a* tick in your ear."

"I don't? That's awesome!"

"You have *three* ticks in your ear. From the looks of it, they've been in there a while, too. Do you ever take showers?"

"Yeah, I took one on…" When I stopped to think about it, I couldn't remember the last time I'd actually taken a shower. Mom always hounds me to take a shower, and I always say I will in a little while, but I usually forget. I couldn't remember the last time I'd actually taken one. "I'm pretty sure I took one a few days ago?"

"I'm not so convinced. You're a bit ripe. Now, stay still."

All of a sudden, Mom appeared. "How's it going out here? You're sister is conscious and feeling calmer."

"Wonderful. Your son has three ticks in his ear, and I haven't even checked his hair yet. For all we know, there's a whole colony in there."

"What! Justin, did you take a shower before we left?"

"No, I didn't have time."

"From what I can smell, he hasn't had a shower in about a week," Mrs. Cliff added.

It was quiet for a few minutes, except for the sound of the cars zooming by like missiles. Mrs. Cliff and Mom checked over my head like mother chimpanzees looking for a wriggly snack.

"Well, that does it. It's just the three in your ear. We'll have to burn them off, of course. I'll go get some matches," Mrs. Cliff said.

"I don't think that's how you're supposed to get them off," Mom said.

I was also pretty sure that's not how you're supposed to get a tick off. It might have been what they did when Mrs. Cliff was young, back in the Dark Ages.

"Well, I'm open to any suggestions," Mrs. Cliff said. "Unfortunately, we don't have the nurse here to help us out. This is pure street medicine. We need to get these ticks off your son's ear and get on our way. We're already way behind schedule."

"Let me look up on my phone how to get a tick off. You go get the matches, please," Mom said.

Mom typed on her phone: *How do you get a tick out of your ear?* She didn't go on an actual medical site but instead went on some lame site where regular people try to answer each other's questions. I tried to tell her to try another site, but she told me to quiet down. I could see the Web page she was reading:

Type Question Here: How do I get a tick out of my ear?

Best Answers – Based On Our Readers

Go To the docter. You shuld be fine. Who knows? —By afternoon doc the wax in your ear will probably kill it. You probably won't die. –By Karen

That's gross!!!! Ticks carry diseases. You're going to get Lyme disease. Good luck!! –By hope it helps

Get it off quick before it gets into your brain. I read somewhere that they like to feed on human brains. Just sayin' –by anonymous

You're in trouble dude!!! My grandma burned a tick off my head with a match once. It worked pretty good, except for the burn. The scar's almost gone. –By happy to be alive

Leave the tick in your ear and let me know how big it gets. –by curious fella

Don't listen to curious fella. If you leave it in your ear you'll lose your hearing and probably die and stuff. Rub toothpaste on the tick. It will suffocate it and then you can brush it out. Make sure you get a new toothbrush after because there'll be tick parts on it. If that doesn't work, I'd just scratch it off with my finger. Can you upload a picture?

Click here for more help

Mom and I looked at each other in disbelief. "I think you should try another Web site," I said.

"We're having a very bad morning," Mom said, ignoring me. "I'm not thrilled about Mrs. Cliff removing the tick with a match, but something tells me that woman's removed a few ticks in her day."

Mrs. Cliff reappeared and lit the first match. She held it for a second and then blew it out. "Tilt your head," she commanded. I did.

With my head tilted, I noticed all the kids on the bus had their faces pressed up against the windows trying to get a look at me. Some of them had cameras and were taking pictures and video. Behind our bus, parked along the highway, were all three coach buses jammed with the rest of the kids in my grade. I could see a bunch of faces on the coaches trying to make out what kind of horror was playing out for me on the shoulder of the highway.

After a few scorching hot pokes, and a tug or sixty from some tweezers that Mrs. Cliff had dug out of her makeup case, she said, "That's all of them. You should be fine."

"I'm not so sure about that," I said.

She looked me in the eyes. "Justin, you're lucky we got them out. Be happy it wasn't worse." She took my hand and pulled to lead me back to the bus.

"Owwww!" I shouted.

"What is it?"

"I have a bite on my hand, and it kills."

"What kind of a bite?"

"It's a snakebite," Mom said under her breath.

"What goes on at your house?" Mrs. Cliff asked.

"I'd rather not get into it right now if it's all right with you, Mrs. Cliff."

"That makes two of us. Justin, get on the bus, now!"

8
Running Late

By the time we got back in our seats and everyone finished asking me how I was doing, it was eight forty-five. The schedule was set for us to be at the Statue of Liberty by nine. Since we had traveled only a few exits, there was no way we were going to be at the statue in time. People were starting to realize it and complain to Mrs. Cliff.

"It's your fault!" Mindy said.

"I wasn't the one who almost dropped dead because of a tiny insect."

"You are a menace," Becky said.

"Thanks. I'm so glad you girls were allowed to join me on my trip. Why'd you even come anyway?"

"We came because we wanted a day off from school," Mindy said, turning to look out the window.

"Yeah!" Becky added, taking out her phone and opening up a game.

"You have your phone on the bus?" I asked.

"No, this is an illusion. Of course I have my phone on the bus."

"We're not allowed to take our phones on the trip. Mrs. Cliff will take it away."

"No, she won't. I'm in middle school, and we're allowed to have our phones.

I knew that Aaron had his phone, even though we weren't supposed to. His parents told him to take it everywhere in case he ever got in an emergency. If you ask me, all kids should have cell phones at all times. Adults are so weird about kids having them, though, which is nuts.

They want us to always be safe and worry about us getting lost, but then they don't want us to have phones. It seems to me that if you want to keep a kid from getting lost, you might want him to have a phone.

Both of my sisters have had phones for a while, and my parents won't even talk to me about getting one.

"Can I borrow it for a minute to text Aaron on the other bus?"

"No way! You'll get me in trouble. I have this for emergency purposes and entertainment."

"Come on. I'll send him one text, and then you can have it right back."

"Give me half your allowance for a month, and I'll consider it."

"That's crazy!"

"So is you asking me to borrow my phone."

"Fine, you can have half my allowance for a month. Jeez! That's totally unfair for one measly text."

She handed me the phone. "You've got a minute."

I quickly texted Aaron: *Hey, how's it going back there? It's me, Justin.*

He texted back a few seconds later: *Better than you!*

No kidding. It's torture in here.

We're watching a movie and lounging in the comfy seats. The seat next to me is totally empty because I was saving it for you! What happened? Kids are saying you have lice.

No, I had a bunch of ticks in my ear from being in the woods.

Gross! I wondered what was going on. I took a picture out the window. It looked like Mrs. Cliff was trying to pull your head off!

He attached a blurry picture of Mrs. Cliff tugging at my ear with those dirty makeup-bag tweezers of hers.

Please delete it!

No chance. This is priceless. Do I have your permission to start a rumor back here that you have bugs in your brain and may have to be flown to the hospital by helicopter?

Sure, whatever. It's not so far from the truth. Some Web site said I probably have Lyme disease. I'm sure my mom—

My sister snatched the phone out of my hand.

"Times up, thunder thumbs."

"Come on! Just a few minutes longer."

"Nope."

9
Restless Parents

At about nine thirty, the bus hit some serious traffic. It was completely stopped for what felt like a lifetime. We couldn't see what was causing the holdup because it was a stretch of cars as far as you could see.

The plan was to be at the Statue of Liberty ferry by nine. Things were not looking too good. I could hear the parents behind me complaining about how poorly the trip had been planned and how they wanted their money back because the kids were promised a coach bus.

One mom walked up to Mrs. Cliff's seat and said, "Mrs. Cliff, we're starting to get worried that the kids aren't going to be able to get in all the day's activities."

"We're going to do our best," Mrs. Cliff said. They continued to talk for a few minutes, but the conversation was so boring I could hardly stand it.

I reached into my backpack and dug out my sandwich. It was kind of soggy and looked like it was sweating from the heat more than I was. I unwrapped it and gave it a sniff.

"You can't eat your lunch on the bus," the mom talking to Mrs. Cliff said to me. I think she was Adam Carlton's mom. Adam was annoying and always telling people what to do. *I guess the apple doesn't fall too far from the tree,* I thought.

"Yeah, you can't eat that," Mindy said.

"Why not?" I asked. "I didn't have any breakfast."

Mom turned around. "Why didn't you have any breakfast?"

"Because I was out in the woods looking for snakes this morning, and I didn't have time."

"We ended up on this stinky old bus because your son was in the woods looking for snakes? What kind of mother doesn't make her kid breakfast on the day of a field trip?" Adam's mom said.

"We had a very tough morning," Mom defended.

"Well, you're not the only one. Everyone on this bus is sweating like animals and uncomfortable because you couldn't get your son here on time."

"It's not my mom's fault," I said.

Mrs. Cliff interrupted. "None of us are happy about being on this bus when the rest of the grade is relaxing in comfort. However, blaming and pointing fingers is not the solution. Please take your seat, Mrs. Carlton."

I was proud of Mrs. Cliff. It was the first time I think I actually liked her. She really put Adam's mom in her place. It's a good thing, too, because I was about to ask her if she picks her nose and eats it like Adam does. That probably wouldn't have gone over very well. Mrs. Carlton made her way back to her seat, but I could hear her grumbling with some of the other moms.

"Go ahead and eat half of your sandwich, Justin," Mom told me. "I don't want you passing out like your sister."

I was about to take my first bite when I felt a flick on my right ear. I turned to flick my sister back and noticed she was asleep. Giggles came from the seat behind me. It was Thomas and Stephen. They loved driving people crazy.

"Cut it out, guys," I said.

"I didn't do anything," Thomas said.

"Me either," Stephen added.

"Just don't do it again," I warned. They giggled.

I was starting to get claustrophobic. I have a really hard time with closed-in places. It's not easy for me to sit still for too long. Being sandwiched between my sisters in the heat for that long was starting to really get to me.

I gobbled down half my sandwich and put the other half back in my bag. There was so much mayo. It was gross. I tried to close my eyes and go to sleep like my sisters. Every time I was about to fall asleep, one of the guys behind us flicked my ear.

10
Bridge Buzz

The teachers decided to start the day at the bridge because we were running so late, and they felt we could use the exercise after all the time on the bus.

By the time we were all off the buses and ready to start our walk across the bridge, it was almost eleven! It had taken us over three hours to travel a distance that should have taken about an hour and a half. Luckily, I ended up falling asleep for the last hour or so. I was so sweaty and gross, and I felt like I had a fever.

"You don't look so good," Mom said when we got off the bus and into the daylight.

"I'm fine," I said.

There were so many other people on their way to walk across the bridge. *How are all these people free on a Friday morning?* I wondered. Each class was ordered to stay together. Each parent had a group of kids to watch out for. I was hoping I could finally see my friends and maybe find Aaron in the sea of people.

Since we almost missed the bus, Mrs. Cliff hadn't assigned Mom any other kids. "Why don't you just look after your own kids?" Mrs. Cliff told her.

I'm pretty sure Mom was insulted, but she didn't say anything. We walked toward the bridge in this gigantic mass of fourth graders. I couldn't believe the teachers were doing this because there was a good chance one of us would get lost. I was secretly hoping it would be Thomas or Stephen.

If you walk fast, you can walk across the bridge in about a half hour. We were moving so slow it was going to take us about a month. Everyone was stopping to take pictures, point at buildings in the distance, and just talk. Mrs. Cliff and the other teachers were like sheepdogs walking around the pack, nipping at our heels, trying to keep us moving forward. I couldn't find Aaron, or any of the guys from my football team, anywhere.

We must have been walking for about ten minutes when the first kid in the group got stung by a bee. It was Shannon Little. She was a few people ahead of me. I saw her swat at something like a crazy person and then start crying. Instantly the kid next to her got stung too. Before I knew it, people were getting stung all around me. Kids started to panic and run in different directions. Mrs. Cliff blew the whistle she had hanging around her neck like a deranged referee. The sound of the whistle seemed to create more panic.

Becky and Mindy both freaked out, of course. They didn't run, though. They stood in place and shrieked. I dug my camera out of my bag and snapped a few pictures of the chaos before I got stung on my neck. It was like being zapped by a laser gun. Before I knew it, I realized there was another one in my shirt. I tried to squash it, but it got me right in the middle of my back. As I was trying to wriggle it out of my shirt, a bee stung me right on the inside of my right nostril.

By the time it was all over, fifteen or twenty kids had been stung. Andrew Chulse ended up with the most bites. He had six in all. It was a complete and total bee freak-out.

For the rest of the walk, my body was throbbing in pain. "I think we have to go to the emergency room," Mom said.

"I'm okay," I told her.

"Justin, today you've been bitten by a snake, had three ticks in your ear, and now you were attacked by bees. There's only so much the human body can take."

"I'm fine," I said.

Clearly, I wasn't fine. I could feel my nose swelling up, and my neck already had a big swollen lump on it. Mrs. Cliff and Mom rubbed some kind of ointment on my stings, which was pretty weird, especially when she was putting it on my nostril. It's a moment I'd like to forget, but it's burned into my brain forever.

While Mrs. Cliff stuck ointment up my nose, Mom finally noticed that the lame sneakers she made me buy were the same exact sneakers Mrs. Cliff was wearing. "I think it's so cute that you two have the same sneakers," she said.

Yeah, this is really cute, I thought.

11
Throbbing

By the time we got to the other side of the bridge, it was one o'clock, and some of us looked like the walking wounded. When we got back on the bus my sister's phone buzzed. She read the text and handed it to me. "Here, no charge this time."

"Thanks," I said, taking the phone. In my reflection off the phone's screen, it was clear that my nose was really ballooning. It looked like I had just lost a heavyweight boxing match.

It was a text from Aaron: *Where were you? I didn't see you on the bridge!*

I texted back: *I was there. I got stung three times. Mrs. Cliff put ointment on me with her stinky old fingers. Did you get stung?*

He texted back: *Man, you're having a bad day. No stings here. Somebody's mom just handed out bags of candy. We're on our way to the Statue of Liberty! I'll see you there.*

Not only was the sting in my nose throbbing, but it itched really bad, too. I must have been scratching it and not paying attention to how far up my nose my finger was going, because from behind me, Stephen shouted, "Nose picker!"

Thomas added, "Finger licker!"

My finger flew back out of my nose instantly. I turned to face them and said, "I wasn't picking. I got a bee sting in my nose. I was just rubbing it!"

"You're a picker," Stephen said, pretending to twist his finger up his nose.

"And a finger licker," Thomas added, pretending to lick his finger.

"I was…" I tried to explain.

"*You was pickin' your schnoz, Justin,*" Stephen interrupted.

"Whatever. You guys know I was just scratching my bee sting. Stop being such *jerks!*" I said. Only, I sort of shouted it.

The bus immediately fell silent. Mrs. Cliff turned around instantly. "We do not use hurtful language in my class," she warned. That's when she spotted the phone in my hand. "I'll take that, Justin."

"Oh, no, this is my sister's."

"Yeah, it's mine," Becky said.

"The phone," Mrs. Cliff insisted.

"But it's my phone," my sister said for the second time.

"I'm not talking to you, dear. Justin, hand me that phone."

"Careful, Mrs. Cliff," Stephen said. "It's covered in boogers."

I handed it to her. Mrs. Cliff scrolled the texts, and from the look on her face, she didn't like what she read. "I'm sorry my stinky old fingers were so bothersome, Justin. I was only trying to help. Trust me when I say I did not plan on sticking my finger up anyone else's nose today." She looked like I'd hurt her feelings.

"I was just kidding around," I said.

Mom looked like she was going to blow her top.

"I was just kidding around," I tried to tell her. I knew she was angry because she was really quiet. When she gets really quiet, it means she's too angry to speak. That would definitely mean big trouble later.

For the moment, though, I was only in trouble with Mrs. Cliff. She asked the driver to use his radio to call one of the other buses.

I heard her say, "Hi, it's Mrs. Cliff. Aaron Wilson on your bus is texting with a child in my class. I've confiscated his phone. Please ask Mrs. Fiesta to do the same."

I felt terrible that Aaron was going to have his phone taken away. Hopefully he wouldn't be mad at me too. My sister was crying hysterically and complaining about how it wasn't fair. Mom told her she shouldn't have had it out in the first place and she could have it back later on.

She got super upset. "All my music is on there. If I don't get it back, I'll go crazy." My sisters are the biggest Jason Freeber fans on the planet. "Mom, I just downloaded his new album this morning. I've only listened to it once. I'll go crazy if I can't listen to it. Please, Mrs. Cliff!"

Mrs. Cliff hardly even looked at her. She was too busy eyeballing every kid she thought might start to misbehave in the back. "Sorry, dear. I'll give it back when we return to the school. The Justin Freeber album will be there later." I thought it was strange that she knew what album Becky was talking about. *Maybe she saw it on Becky's phone,* I thought.

Mrs. Cliff was looking like she had had about enough field trip fun for one day. The bus was making its way downtown to reach the ferry terminal for the Statue of Liberty. Some of the kids on the bus were singing "Ninety-Nine Bottles of Beer on the Wall," which Mrs. Cliff clearly did not like. I couldn't believe that most of the parents were singing it too. Mom did not look happy.

They were down to seventy-nine bottles of beer on the wall when one of the front tires burst and the bus swerved hard to the right and rolled over a fire hydrant, which popped off and bounced down the street. The bus was stopped directly on top of the hydrant opening, which was gushing water. We couldn't see it at first because the water was hitting the bottom of the bus. You could hear it, though. It sounded like, well, a fire hydrant spraying the bottom of the bus. It was really loud. Water was all over the street outside, making puddles and small streams rolling in all directions.

Mrs. Cliff blew her whistle again. I'm not sure why because it just made everyone panic even more. The bus driver hit the alarm, so the bus was blinking and bleeping like a spastic yellow robot. She rushed to the back of the bus and threw open the emergency escape door. We'd done the drill where you sit and hop out of the back of the bus a million times at school, but I never dreamed I would actually ever need to do it.

One of the dads was trying to prop open the escape hatch in the ceiling when the bus driver told him to stop and come out the back with the rest of us. Watching the parents hop out the back was pretty funny. It was such a scene. There was water all over the place and people freaking out about the flat tire. We were all the way in the front, so I knew we'd be some of the last people off. Kids and parents jammed into the aisle waiting to jump out the back.

One of the parents said, "Can't we simply go out the front doors?"

"We're going out the back," Mrs. Cliff told her firmly.

Mindy and Becky jumped off, landed, and walked to the sidewalk where the rest of the group was. Mrs. Cliff insisted Mom go first. She agreed. Then it was my time. I'd done the back-door jump a zillion times before. I didn't sit on my tush like I was some kind of little kid. I walked close to the edge and jumped, or at least tried to jump. Unfortunately for me, my ridiculous sneakers got caught on something, and I tripped. I tumbled out of the bus like a bag of laundry and fell face-first into a dirty city puddle.

12
911

A bus full of kids crashed into a fire hydrant brings more firefighters and police than I ever could have imagined possible. Every car and truck with a flashing emergency light in the city must have been sent to save us.

We watched from the sidewalk as they towed the bus off the gushing water and shut off the water supply. We watched as they repaired the flat tire on the bus. By the time the tire was repaired and the bus was ready to go, it was three o'clock, and the other classes were already at the statue.

An ambulance lady insisted on checking out every single person involved in the bus crash. When she got a look at me and all my bites and wet clothes, she ordered that I be taken to the hospital. Mom tried telling her that I was fine, but the woman wasn't having it any other way.

"You ruined today," Becky told me.

"Thanks," I said.

"Your brother didn't ruin anything. Today was doomed from the moment we woke up. We need to go to the hospital, get checked out, and just go home."

The lady checked out the rest of the kids and then carted my sisters, my mom, and me off to the hospital. Mom told Mrs. Cliff that we'd probably take the train home after the hospital.

The ambulance ride was the best part of the day. The driver was going really fast and zig-zagging in and out of traffic. When we got to the hospital, they insisted on putting me on a stretcher and wheeling me in the big entrance door. It seemed like a whole lot of drama for a couple of bug bites.

At the hospital, we were in the ER, which stands for Emergency Room. The room wasn't really a room at all. It was just a shiny metal-framed bed surrounded by a bunch of curtains. We were in the corner room all the way in the back, but I could hear all the other people in the ER talking and making noise. There was a little kid who was about five crying because they wanted to take his blood pressure.

We sat in the room for a while waiting to see the doctor. The girls were still giving me the silent treatment, and Mom was exhausted.

After a while, the doctor, whose name was Igor, arrived. He had an accent that sounded like he was from Transylvania. He checked me over and said, "We'll need to take some blood to check for da Lyme disease." And the way he said "take some blood" reminded me so much of the count from *Sesame Street* that I started laughing.

Becky finally spoke. "This is just too weird."

The doctor said, "I assure you, I'm not a vampire. I only sound like one." Then he put his doctor coat over the bottom of his face, like a vampire would with a cape, and said, "Don't move a muscle. I'll be back!"

When he was out of earshot, Mindy said, "Where are we?"

"This place gives me the creeps," Becky said.

"I really just want to get you checked out and get home. Today is getting weirder by the minute," Mom said.

We could hear a bunch of people rushing into the room right next to us. There were so many people in the room that our curtain kept getting pushed back. We could hear them talking as if they were in the room with us. We had to listen to what they were saying. There was no other choice.

A woman's voice said, "He'll be fine. We just need to ice it."

A guy said, "There's no time for ice. We need to get him on his feet and get him to the show."

We were all listening carefully to what was going on. It sounded very important. The guy and the girl argued back and forth about someone. They mentioned the word "perform" a few times.

Finally, a boy said, "I'm fine, really. It's a bit sore, but I can still perform." His voice sounded kind of familiar, but I couldn't place it.

Becky and Mindy grabbed each other's hands and made faces like they were screaming but didn't make any sound.

"What?" I said.

13
Jason Freeber!

"That's Jason Freeber!" Mindy whispered.

"No way," I said, reaching out to pull back the curtain for a look.

They both grabbed me. "Don't look, but it's totally him," Mindy said.

"I can't believe this," Becky added. "I'm finally close to Jason Freeber, and I'm in a gross hospital with my bug-infested brother."

"Cut that out," Mom warned.

We kept on listening to what they were saying. It sounded like he had twisted his ankle.

"Either way," a new voice said, "he's got to take the stage at five, or we'll have to cancel."

I looked at my watch. It was four fifteen.

"Thanks to you, I don't have my phone! I can't even take a picture with him!" Becky said.

She was right. Mom had a phone with her, but Mom's phone was pretty lame and didn't have a camera.

The girls were really excited. They were also crowded around Mom's small makeup mirror, fixing their hair and making themselves as pretty as possible under the conditions.

Every time he spoke, the girls looked like they were going to shoot right through the ceiling with excitement. We heard him say, "It's just my ankle. It hurts so much. These shoes aren't going to work."

"We don't have time to go find a different pair of shoes," one of the voices said.

"Can you perform barefoot?" another asked.

Mom grabbed my wrist and pointed to my all-white, extra-big-heeled sneakers. The girls jumped up and down and whispered, "*Yes!*"

Before I could say a word, Becky pulled back the curtain and said, "Jason, I think we have a solution to your problem." She also flipped her head to the side to create dramatic hair movement.

His people tried to close the curtain on her, but he told them to stop. Jason was sitting on a bed just like mine. He was a few years older than me, but he was really small for his age.

"What are you talking about?" he asked.

The girls froze up. I hopped off the bed and said, "Jason, my mom bought me these horribly lame sneakers for back-to-school last week because they make me look 'sturdy on your feet,' whatever that means. If you want to try them, they might help your ankle."

"Those are pretty cool!" he said.

"Seriously?" I asked.

"I picked them out," Becky chirped.

"I helped," Mindy managed.

"You really think these are cool?" I asked.

"Yeah, especially since you girls helped pick them out," he said to Mindy and Becky. If he were in front of a big crowd of fans, that would have been the part when all the girls let out a loud, high-pitched scream. I thought the girls might, but instead they went, "Awwwww."

"You've got to be careful in them because the heel is so big," I interrupted. The girls were starting to gross me out. "I've wiped out a bunch of times already, but if you take it slow, they do give you a lot of support."

"Justin, that's the nicest thing anyone has said to me all day!" Mom said. "That's what I've been telling you all week. You've just been walking lazy."

I untied them and held them out for Jason. "They're all yours if you want to try them."

The people with him were all whispering into cell phones and texting away like crazy. The woman who seemed to be in charge said, "Try them on and see if they help your ankle."

Jason tried them on and gently hopped off the bed.

"You look so sturdy on your feet!" Mom said.

"They look super cute," Mindy said.

Jason gave her his cutest pop star smile and said, "Thanks, Mindy."

"He knows my name! You know my name!"

Both of my sisters squeaked and giggled like I've never heard before.

"They feel pretty good. The ankle still hurts, but they're sturdy. I feel like I'm walking on air."

The woman in charge asked me, "How much?"

"We can't take your money," Mom said. "Just return them when you're done. Justin can wear Mr. Freeber's shoes for the rest of the day."

"Perfect," Jason said. "Let's get going. The show starts in about thirty minutes."

"What show?" I asked.

"I'm playing a free show in Times Square at five o'clock."

"We thought we might have to cancel," an important-looking man said.

"That's so weird," I said. "My class is sched-
uled to go to Times Square at about five o'clock."

"You're welcome to ride with us over there
and be our guests at the show," the man said.

"That sounds awesome," I said. "Jason, how
do you feel about taking my sisters onstage with
you?" I asked.

"It'd be my pleasure to invite Mindy and
Becky onstage with me, Justin," he said, doing his
trademark hair flip, "if you girls are interested."

They could only jump up and down. I think
they managed a little nodding too. I couldn't
help thinking Jason must have been given some
kind of special training that helped him remember names. It was definitely a good trick because
he made us all feel like he knew us, even though
we had only met a few minutes before.

Mom went out to track down Igor and tell
him we were leaving and that she'd take me to
the doctor first thing in the morning. I told
Becky I didn't owe her half my allowance any-
more. She agreed.

14
Best Trip Ever!

We were all hurried out a back door of the hospital and into these big black trucks. The girls both got to sit next to Jason, and he was the one squished in the middle for a change. We zoomed through city traffic like it was nothing because we had a police escort. I couldn't believe it. You would have thought it was the Queen of England or the president the way the police were clearing the way for the kid.

The cars pulled right into the center of Times Square. We got out and were ushered to the stage. Before I knew what was going on, Jason was on the stage, and the crowd was going nuts.

"I almost didn't make it here for the show," he announced. "I fell and hurt my ankle pretty bad earlier today, but at the hospital, I met a few new friends who helped me out. My new buddy Justin hooked me up with these awesome sneakers." He lifted his right foot up so everyone could see them. The crowd cheered.

Mom leaned in close to me and whispered, "Turns out I'm not so lame!"

I laughed, "I guess not. Maybe Jason should hire you to be his stylist?"

Jason shouted, "Are you ready to rock?"

The crowd went crazy again. My sisters were out of their minds with excitement. He waved for them to come out, and his band went into their hit single "Love, Puppy, Baby." The girls ran out onstage with Jason and danced their faces off.

Mom and I watched from the back of the stage. Her phone buzzed. "Hello," she shouted over the music. "Hi, Mrs. Cliff. Justin is just fine. Thanks for checking in. Where are we? We're in Times Square, at the Jason Freeber concert. Don't ask. It's a long story." She paused to listen to Mrs. Cliff. "You guys are in Times Square too? You see the girls?" She put her hand over the phone and whispered to me, "They can see the girls!" Then she talked into the phone again. "We'll talk to you guys after the concert!"

15
Mrs. Cliff = Mrs. Cool?

I'm not a big pop music fan, but I have to admit, Jason Freeber can really put on a show. He danced, played the guitar, and got Times Square filled with energy. It was a great time. I'd almost forgotten about my swollen nose and snake bitten hand when the girls came running offstage.

"That was the greatest thing that ever happened to me!" Mindy said.

"Me too," Becky added. "Thanks, Justin."

"Yeah," Mindy said. "You really came through on this one."

"Thanks, girls!" I couldn't believe how nice they were being to me. My sisters and I are usually in battle with each other over the smallest little things. It was kind of cool to get along for a change.

"Why don't we find your class and figure out how we're going to get home." Mom said.

"Get this," Mindy said. "Jason said he would have one of his drivers take us home!"

"Wow!" Mom said. "This day just keeps getting better and better. Let's go find Mrs. Cliff and let her know."

Mom called Mrs. Cliff, and we walked through the crowd and found my class. All the girls on the trip swarmed my sisters. They had just lived every girl's dream come true.

"You looked so cool up there," one girl said to them.

"That was the most amazing thing I've ever seen!" another girl said.

Mrs. Cliff appeared out of nowhere. "Hi, Justin," she said. I couldn't believe my eyes.

Mrs. Cliff looked all sweaty, as if she'd been dancing, and she was wearing a Jason Freeber shirt and matching headband!

"Mrs. Cliff? What are you doing all Freebered out?"

"I'm a *huge* Freeber fan! Why do you think I planned to end our day in Times Square today? I knew about this free concert months ago. Isn't he the cat's meow?"

I had no idea what that meant, but I said, "Yeah...I guess." Then I had a brilliant idea. "Mrs. Cliff, would you like to meet Jason Freeber?"

It was perfect. She was a huge fan, and he was my new BFF! She and I walked back to the stage. His security guys let me and Mrs. Cliff go right back to see him. We went backstage where he was sitting.

"Hey, Jason," I said.

He was texting. He stopped and said, "Hey, Justin! These sneakers rocked! I hardly felt any pain." He looked down at Mrs. Cliff's sneakers. "You've got the same ones!"

"Yeah!" Mrs. Cliff yelped excitedly. "I love the big heel. I think they're super cool!"

"May I ask your name, young lady?"

Mrs. Cliff blushed. "I'm hardly a young lady. But you sure are sweet! I'm Justin's teacher. We ended our field trip today by seeing you."

"I really appreciate that, Mrs. Cliff."

"I'm a *huge* fan!"

"That's awesome. Why don't we take a picture, and I'll have my assistant e-mail it to you?"

Jason and Mrs. Cliff took a few pictures together, he signed her shirt and headband, and apparently, I was Mrs. Cliff's new favorite student. This trip was turning out way better than I had expected.

16
Skunked

Before we climbed into the car to head back home, Mrs. Cliff actually gave me a hug. It was a pretty amazing turnaround. A week ago, I was easily her least favorite student, and now I was her hero. Go figure.

As our car pulled away, she shouted, "Don't forget that we have our first social studies test on Tuesday! Remember to study..."

The word "study" sort of drifted away behind us. *Why'd she have to go and ruin a perfectly good ending like that?* I wondered.

"You didn't tell me you have a test on Tuesday," Mom said. The guy driving the car smiled and laughed to himself.

"Does Jason Freeber have to deal with this on a Friday night?" I asked.

"No," he laughed. "He does not."

Maybe I should start taking singing and dancing lessons, I thought.

"Justin," Mom said, "on a more positive note, the girls and I were talking, and they have something they'd like to say to you."

"We're sorry we were so happy when you had to give away Mr. Squeeze last week," Mindy said.

"Yeah, that wasn't cool," Becky added.

"Your sisters asked me if your father and I will consider giving you another chance with Mr. Squeeze."

"*Really?* Thank you, guys! That's amazing."

It was pretty amazing. A week ago, my sisters couldn't get rid of that snake fast enough. Now, thanks to pop icon Jason Freeber, Mr. Squeeze was as good as saved.

"What do you say, Mom?" I asked, flashing her my best Jason Freeber smile.

"I texted your father, and he agreed that we can give you another chance, but you have to promise to be more careful with that lid! We don't want a boa constrictor getting loose in the house again."

"I'll make sure he can't get out! You guys are awesome!"

It was by far the single greatest day I've ever had with my mom and sisters. We laughed and talked the whole ride home. It was like a scene out of some cheesy movie where everything just magically works out perfect in the end. Unfortunately, this wasn't a movie, and the night did not end perfectly.

Things went sour around ten o'clock, when I was lying in bed. I was thinking about how awesome it would be to get Mr. Squeeze back in the morning when I heard a super loud, ear-bending shriek fill the house. It was Mom!

I bolted out of bed and ran to Mom and Dad's room. The lights were on, and they were both standing up on chairs. "There's a *snake* in our *bed*!"

That's when I remembered the Garter snake I'd caught that morning. I guess that lid wasn't strong enough to keep a snake in the tank. It was curled up right in the middle of their bed. I jumped on it and grabbed it with two hands so I wouldn't get bitten again. It wriggled around for a few seconds. As I was wrestling with it, Mindy and Becky ran into the room. They immediately freaked and jumped up on the chairs with Mom and Dad.

When Garter snakes get scared, they can sometimes release this awful-smelling spray. It's a defense mechanism, kind of like a skunk's. This snake must have been really scared because it sprayed me and Mom and Dad's bed.

"What is that?" Dad asked. The girls and Mom were coughing and covering their mouths and noses.

It smelled absolutely horrible. My eyes were watering it was so bad. All I could think to say was, "Can I still keep Mr. Squeeze?"

It was a perfectly horrible end to a perfectly horrible day.

Look for the next book in the series
School Is A Nightmare #3
Coming Summer 2012
Sign up for an email alert at
raymondbeanbooks@gmail.com or visit
www.raymondbean.com

Made in the USA
Charleston, SC
21 August 2013